Bill with a Will

by: CLAYBIGMAC

Gotham Books
30 N Gould St.
Ste. 20820, Sheridan, WY 82801
https://gothambooksinc.com/

Phone: 1 (307) 464-7800

© 2022 Claybigmac. All rights reserved.
No part of this book may be reproduced, stored in a
retrieval system, or transmitted by any means without the
written permission of the author.

Published by Gotham Books (November 10, 2022)

ISBN: 979-8-88775-125-2 (sc)
ISBN: 979-8-88775-126-9 (e)

Because of the dynamic nature of the Internet, any web
addresses or links contained in this book may have changed
since publication and may no longer be valid.

The views expressed in this work are solely those of the
author and do not necessarily reflect the views of the
publisher, and the publisher hereby disclaims any responsibility for them.

HEROES

To my family - you are the inspiration of my life. Everyone of you has as special place in my heart. I feel so blessed to be a part of your lives and to walk with you in this woderful world.

Thank you for showing me that....

"Happiness begins in the Heart!" ~ Claybigmac

"I'm Bill, I'm Bill, Bill with a will.
A will, a will, that's why I'm called Bill."

"Making it home long before tea.
I can! I can! It`s what gives me a thrill."

"What makes us tick? How is it so?
Running around, staying on the go."

"You never quit, for quitters don't win.
I smile and tell Poppy, with a great grin."

"But with a will, it gives you a chance.
To show how you feel and then make a stance."

Reflection Time

1. Why is it ok to start over again if we fail?

   Answer: _____

2. What do you do if something does not go your way?

   Answer: _____

3. How do you think Bill would respond if something did not go his way?

   Answer: _____

4. What makes you feel happy inside?

   Answer: _____

5. Do you know something that you could help others to do - What is it?

   Answer: _____

"Happiness begins in the Heart!" ~ Claybigmac